THE
ICE DRAGON
E. NESBIT

Pictures by
Carole Gray

Dial Books for Young Readers
NEW YORK

This is the tale of the wonders that befell on the evening of the 11th December, when they did what they were told not to do. You may think that you know all the unpleasant things that could possibly happen to you if you are disobedient, but there are some things which even you do not know, and they did not know them either.

Their names were George and Jane.

There were no fireworks that year on Guy Fawkes' day, because the heir to the throne was not well. He was cutting his first tooth, and that is a very anxious time for any person — even for a Royal one. He was really very poorly, so that fireworks would have been in the worst possible taste, even at Land's End or in the Isle of Man, whilst in Forest Hill, which was the home of Jane and George, anything of the kind was quite out of the question. Even the Crystal Palace, empty-headed as it is, felt that this was no time for catherine-wheels.

But when the Prince had cut his tooth, rejoicings were not only admissible but correct, and the 11th December was proclaimed firework day. All the people were most anxious to show their loyalty, and to enjoy themselves at the same time. So there were fireworks and torchlight processions, and set-pieces at the Crystal Palace, with 'Blessings on our Prince' and 'Long Live our Royal Darling' in different coloured fires; and the most private of boarding schools had a half-holiday; and even the children of plumbers and authors had tuppence each given them to spend as they liked.

George and Jane had sixpence each — and they spent the whole amount on a 'golden rain', which would not light for ever so long, and, when it did light, went out almost at once, so they had to look at the fireworks in the gardens next door, and the ones at the Crystal Palace, which were very glorious indeed.

All their relations had colds in their heads, so Jane and George were allowed to go out into the garden alone to let off their firework. Jane had to put on her fur cape and her thick gloves, and her hood with the silver-fox fur on it which was made out of mother's old muff; and George had his overcoat with the three capes, and his comforter, and father's sealskin travelling cap with the pieces that come down over your ears.

It was very dark in the garden, but the fireworks all about made it seem very gay, and though the children were very cold they were quite sure that they were enjoying themselves.

They got up on the fence at the end of the garden to see better; and then they saw, very far away, where the edge of the dark world is, a shining line of straight, beautiful lights arranged in a row, as if they were the spears carried by a fairy army.

"Oh, how pretty," said Jane. "I wonder what they are. It looks as if the fairies were planting little shining baby poplar trees, and watering them with liquid light."

"Liquid fiddlestick!" said George. He had been to school, so he knew that these were only the aurora borealis, or northern lights. And he said so.

"But what *is* the rory bory what's-its-name?" asked Jane. "Who lights it, and what's it there for?"

George had to own that he had not learnt that.

"But I know," said he, "that it has something to do with the Great Bear, and the Dipper, and the Plough, and Charles's Wain."

"And what are they?" asked Jane.

"Oh, they're the surnames of some of the star families. There goes a jolly rocket," answered George, and Jane felt as if she almost understood about the star families.

The fairy spears of light twinkled and gleamed: they were much prettier than the big, blaring, blazing bonfire that was smoking and flaming and spluttering in the next-door-but-one garden — prettier even than the coloured fires at the Crystal Palace.

"I wish we could see them nearer," Jane said. "I wonder if the star families are nice families — the kind that mother would like us to go to tea with, if we were little stars?"

"They aren't that sort of families at all, silly," said her brother, kindly trying to explain. "I only said 'families' because a kid like you wouldn't have understood if I'd said constel . . . and, besides, I've forgotten the end of the word. Anyway, the stars are all up in the sky, so you can't go to tea with them."

"No," said Jane, "I said if we were little stars."

"But we aren't," said George.

"No," said Jane, with a sigh. "I know that. I'm not so stupid as you think, George. But the tory bories are somewhere at the edge. Couldn't we go and see *them?*"

"Considering you're eight, you haven't much sense." George kicked his boots against the paling to warm his toes. "It's half the world away."

"It looks very near," said Jane, hunching up her shoulders to keep her neck warm.

"They're close to the North Pole," said George. "Look here — I don't care a straw about the aurora borealis, but I shouldn't mind discovering the North Pole: it's awfully difficult and dangerous, and then you come home and write a book about it with a lot of pictures, and everybody says how brave you are."

Jane got off the fence.

"Oh, George, let's," she said. "We shall never have such a chance again — all alone by ourselves — and quite late, too."

"I'd go right enough if it wasn't for you," George answered, gloomily, "but you know they always say I lead you into mischief — and if we went to the North Pole we should get our boots wet, as likely as not, and you remember what they said about not going on the grass."

"They said the *lawn*," said Jane. "We're not going on the *lawn*. Oh, George, do, *do* let's. It doesn't look so *very* far — we could be back before they had time to get dreadfully angry."

"All right," said George, "but mind *I* don't want to go."

So off they went. They got over the fence, which was very cold and white and shiny because it was beginning to freeze, and on the other side of the fence was somebody else's garden, so they got out of that as quickly as they could, and beyond that was a field where there was another big bonfire, with people standing round it who looked quite black.

"It's like Indians," said George, and wanted to stop and look, but Jane pulled him on, and they passed by the bonfire and got through a gap in the hedge into another field — a dark one; and far away, beyond quite a number of other dark fields, the northern lights shone and sparkled and twinkled.

7

Now, during the winter the Arctic regions come much farther south than they are marked on the map. Very few people know this, though you would think they could tell it by the ice in the jugs of a morning. And just when George and Jane were starting for the North Pole, the Arctic regions had come down nearly as far as Forest Hill, so that, as the children walked on, it grew colder and colder, and presently they saw that the fields were covered with snow, and there were great icicles hanging from all the hedges and gates. And the northern lights still seemed some way off.

They were crossing a very rough, snowy field when Jane first noticed the animals. There were rabbits and white hares, and all sorts and sizes of white birds, and some larger creatures in the shadows of the hedges which Jane was sure were wolves and bears.

''Polar bears and Arctic wolves, of course I mean,'' she said, for she did not want George to think her stupid again.

There was a great hedge at the end of this field, all covered with snow and icicles; but the children found a place where there was a hole, and as no bears or wolves seemed to be in just that part of the hedge, they crept through and scrambled out of the frozen ditch on the other side. And then they stood still and held their breath in wonder.

For in front of them, running straight and smooth right away to the northern lights, lay a great wide road of pure dark ice, and on each side were tall trees all sparkling with white frost, and from the boughs

8

of the
trees hung
strings of stars
threaded on fine
moonbeams, and
shining so brightly that
it was like a beautiful fairy
daylight. Jane said so; but
George said it was like the electric
lights at the Earl's Court Exhibition.
The rows of trees went straight as ruled
lines away — and away and away — and at
the other end of them shone the aurora borealis.

There was a signpost — of silvery snow — and on it in letters of pure ice the children read:

"This way to the North Pole."

Then George said: "Way or no way, I know a slide when I see one — so here goes." And he took a run on the frozen snow, and Jane took a run when she saw him do it, and the next moment they were sliding away, each with feet half a yard apart, along the great slide that leads to the North Pole.

This great slide is made for the convenience of the polar bears, who, during the winter months, get their food from the Army and Navy Stores — and it is the most perfect slide in the world. If you have never come across it, it is because you have never been thoroughly naughty and disobedient. But do not be these things in the hope of finding the great slide — because you might find something quite different, and then you would be sorry.

The great slide is like common slides in this, that when once you have started you have to go on to the end — unless you fall down — and then it hurts just as much as the smaller kind on ponds. The great slide runs downhill all the way, so that you keep on going faster and faster and faster. George and Jane went so fast that they had no time to notice the scenery. They only saw the long lines of frosted trees and the starry lamps, and, on each side, rushing back as they slid on — a very broad, white world and a very large, black night; and overhead, as well as in the trees, the stars were bright like silver lamps, and, far ahead, shone and trembled and sparkled the line of fairy spears. Jane said so; and George said, "I can see the northern lights quite plain."

It is very pleasant to slide and slide on clear, dark ice — especially if you feel you are really going somewhere, and more especially if that somewhere is the North Pole. The children's feet made no noise on the ice, and they went on and on in a beautiful white silence. But suddenly the silence was shattered and a cry rang out over the snow.

"Hi! You there! Stop!"

"Tumble for your life!" cried George, and he fell down at once, because it was the only way to stop. Jane fell on top of him — and then they crawled on hands and knees to the snow at the edge of the slide — and there was a sportsman, dressed in a peaked cap and a frozen moustache, like the one you see in the pictures about Ice-Peter, and he had a gun in his hand.

"You don't happen to have any bullets about you?" said he.

"No," George said, truthfully. "I had five of father's revolver cartridges, but they were taken away the day nurse turned out my pockets to see if I had taken the knob of the bathroom door by mistake."

"Quite so," said the sportsman, "these accidents will occur. You don't carry firearms, then, I presume?"

"I haven't got any fire*arms*," said George, "but I have a fire*work*. It's only a squib one of the boys gave me, if that's any good," and he began to feel among the string, and peppermints, and buttons, and tops, and nibs, and chalk, and foreign postage-stamps, in his knickerbocker pockets.

"One could but try," the sportsman replied, and he held out his hand.

But Jane pulled at her brother's jacket-tail, and whispered, "Ask him what he wants it for."

So then the sportsman had to confess that he wanted the firework to kill the white grouse with; and, when they came to look, there was the white grouse himself, sitting in the snow, looking quite pale and careworn, and waiting anxiously for the matter to be decided one way or the other.

George put all the things back in his pockets, and said, "No I shan't. The season for shooting him stopped yesterday — I heard father say so — so it wouldn't be fair, anyhow. I'm very sorry; but I can't — so there!"

The sportsman said nothing, only he shook his fist at Jane, then he got on the slide and tried to go towards the Crystal Palace — which was not easy, because that way is uphill. So they left him trying, and went on.

Before they started the white grouse thanked them in a few pleasant, well-chosen words, and then they took a sideways slanting run, and started off again on the great slide, and so away towards the North Pole and the twinkling, beautiful lights.

The great slide went on and on, and the white silence wrapped them round as they slid along the wide, icy path. Then once again the silence was broken to bits by someone calling: "Hi! You there! Stop!"

"Tumble for your life!" cried George, and tumbled as before, stopping in the only possible way, and Jane stopped on top of him, and they crawled to the edge, and came suddenly on the butterfly collector who was looking for specimens with a pair of blue glasses, and a blue net, and a blue book with coloured plates.

"Excuse me," said the collector, "but have you any such thing as a needle about you — a very long needle?"

"I have a needle-*book*," replied Jane, politely, "but there aren't any needles in it now. George took them all to do the things with pieces of cork — in the *Boy's Own Scientific Experimenter* and the *Young Mechanic*. He did not do the things, but he did for the needles."

"Curiously enough," said the collector, "I, too, wished to use the needle in connection with cork."

"I have a hatpin in my hood," said Jane. "I fastened the fur with it when it caught in the nail on the greenhouse door. It is very long and sharp — would that do?"

"One could but try," said the collector, and Jane began to feel for the pin. But George pinched her arm and whispered, "Ask what he wants it for." Then the collector had to own that he wanted the pin to stick through the great Arctic moth. "A magnificent specimen," he added, "which I am most anxious to preserve."

And there, sure enough, in the collector's butterfly-net sat the great Arctic moth listening attentively to the conversation.

"Oh, I couldn't!" cried Jane. And while George was explaining to the collector that they would really rather not, Jane opened the blue folds of the butterfly-net, and asked the moth, quietly, if it would please step

outside for a moment. And it did. When the collector saw that the moth was free, he seemed less angry than grieved.

"Well, well," said he, "here's a whole Arctic expedition thrown away! I shall have to go home and fit out another. And that means a lot of writing to the papers and things. You seem to be a singularly thoughtless little girl."

So they went on, leaving him, too, trying to go uphill towards the Crystal Palace. When the great Arctic moth had returned thanks in a suitable speech, George and Jane took a sideways slanting run and started sliding again, between the star-lamps along the great slide, towards the North Pole. They went faster and faster, and the lights ahead grew brighter and brighter — so that they could not keep their eyes open, but had to blink as they went — and then suddenly the great slide ended in an immense heap of snow, and George and Jane shot right into it because they could not stop themselves, and the snow was soft so that they went in up to their very ears.

When they picked themselves out, and thumped each other on the back to get rid of the snow, they shaded their eyes and looked, and there, right in front of them, was the wonder of wonders — the North Pole — towering high and white and glistening, like an ice-lighthouse, and it was quite, quite close, so that you had to put your head as far back as it would go, and farther, before you could see the high top of it. It was made entirely of ice. You will hear grown-up people talk a great deal of nonsense about the North Pole, and when you are grown-up, it is even possible that you may talk nonsense about it yourself (the most unlikely things do happen); but deep down in your heart you must always remember that the North Pole is made of clear ice, and could not possibly, if you come to think about it, be made of anything else.

All round the Pole, making a bright ring around it, were hundreds of little fires, and the flames of them did not flicker and twist, but went up blue and green and rosy and straight like the stalks of dream lilies.

Jane said so, but George said they were as straight as ramrods.

And these flames were the aurora borealis — which the children had seen as far away as Forest Hill.

The ground was quite flat, and covered with smooth, hard snow, which shone and sparkled like the top of a birthday cake which has been made at home. The ones done at the shops do not shine and sparkle, because they mix flour with the icing-sugar.

"It is like a dream," said Jane.

And George said, "It *is* the North Pole. Just think of the fuss people always make about getting here — and it was no trouble at all, really."

"I daresay lots of people have *got* here," said Jane, dismally; "it's not the getting *here* — I see that — it's the getting back again. Perhaps no one will

16

ever know that we have been here, and the robins will cover us with leaves
and —''

"Nonsense," said George, "there aren't any robins, and there aren't any
leaves. It's just the North Pole, that's all, and I've found it; and now I shall
try to climb up and plant the British flag on the top — my handkerchief will
do; and if it really *is* the North Pole, my pocket-compass Uncle James gave
me will spin round and round, and then I shall know. Come on."

So Jane came on; and when they got close to the clear, tall, beautiful flames, they saw that there was a great, queer-shaped lump of ice all round the bottom of the Pole — clear, smooth, shining ice, that was deep, beautiful Prussian blue, like icebergs, in the thick parts, and all sorts of wonderful, glimmery, shimmery, changing colours in the thin parts, like the cut-glass chandelier in grandmamma's house in London.

"It's a very curious shape," said Jane; "it's almost like" — she drew back a step to get a better view of it — "it's almost like a *dragon*."

"It's much more like the lampposts on the Thames Embankment," said George, who had noticed a curly thing like a tail that went twisting up the North Pole.

"Oh, George," cried Jane, "it *is* a dragon; I can see its wings. Whatever shall we do?"

And, sure enough, it *was* a dragon — a great, shining, winged, scaly, clawy, big-mouthed dragon — made of pure ice. It must have gone to sleep curled round the hole where the warm steam used to come up from the middle of the Earth, and then when the Earth got colder, and the column of steam froze and was turned into the North Pole, the dragon must have got frozen in his sleep — frozen too hard to move — and there he stayed. And though he was very terrible he was very beautiful, too.

Jane said so, but George said, "Oh, don't bother; I'm thinking how to get on to the Pole and try the compass without waking the brute."

The dragon certainly was beautiful, with his deep, clear Prussian-blueness, and his rainbow—coloured glitter. And rising from within the cold coil of the

frozen
dragon the
North Pole shot
up like a pillar made
of one great diamond,
and every now and then it
cracked a little, from sheer
coldness. The sound of the
cracking was the only thing that broke
the great white silence in the midst of
which the dragon lay like an enormous jewel,
and the straight flames went up all round him like
the stalks of tall lilies.

And as the children stood there looking at the most
wonderful sight their eyes had ever seen, there was a soft
padding of feet and a hurry-scurry behind them, and from the
outside darkness beyond the flame-stalks came a crowd of little
brown creatures running, jumping, scrambling, tumbling head over heels,
and on all fours, and some even walking on their heads. They caught hands as
they came near the fires, and danced round in a ring.

"It's bears," said Jane. "I know it is. Oh, how I wish we hadn't come; and my boots are so wet."

The dancing-ring broke up suddenly, and the next moment hundreds of furry arms clutched at George and Jane, and they found themselves in the middle of a great, soft heaving crowd of little fat people in brown fur dresses, and the white silence was quite gone.

"Bears, indeed," cried a shrill voice; "you'll wish we *were* bears before you've done with us."

This sounded so dreadful, that Jane began to cry. Up to now the children had only seen the most beautiful and wondrous things, but now they began to be sorry they had done what they were told not to, and the difference between 'lawn' and 'grass' did not seem so great as it had done at Forest Hill.

Directly Jane began to cry, all the brown people started back. No one cries in the Arctic regions for fear of being struck so by the frost. So that these people had never seen anyone cry before.

"Don't cry *really*," whispered George, "or you'll get chilblains in your eyes. But *pretend* to howl — it frightens them."

So Jane went on pretending to howl, and the real crying stopped: it always does when you begin to pretend. You try it.

Then, speaking very loud so as to be heard over the howls of Jane, George said: "Yah — who's afraid? We are George and Jane — who are you?"

"We are the sealskin dwarfs," said the brown people, twisting their furry bodies in and out of the crowd like the changing glass in kaleidoscopes. "We are very precious and expensive, for we are made, throughout, of the very best sealskin."

"And what are those fires for?" bellowed George — for Jane was crying louder and louder.

"Those," shouted the dwarfs, coming a step nearer, "are the fires we make to thaw the dragon. He is frozen now — so he sleeps curled up round the Pole — but when we have thawed him with our fires he will wake up and go and eat everybody in the world except us."

"Whatever-do-you-want-him-to-do-that-for?" yelled George.

"Oh — just for spite," bawled the dwarfs, carelessly — as if they were saying, "just for fun."

Jane left off crying to say: "You *are* heartless."

"No, we aren't," they said. "Our hearts are made of the finest sealskin, just like little fat sealskin purses —"

And they all came a step nearer. They were very fat and round. Their bodies were like sealskin jackets on a very stout person; their heads were like sealskin muffs; their legs were like sealskin boas; and their hands and feet were like sealskin tobacco-pouches. And their faces were like seals' faces, inasmuch as they, too, were covered with sealskin.

"Thank you so much for telling us," said George. "Good evening. (Keep on howling, Jane!)"

But the dwarfs came a step nearer, muttering and whispering. Then the muttering stopped — and there was a silence so deep that Jane was afraid to howl in it. But it was a brown silence, and she had liked the white silence better. Then the chief dwarf came quite close and said: "What's that on your head?"

And George felt it was all up — for he knew it was his father's sealskin cap.

The dwarf did not wait for an answer. "It's made from one of *us*," he screamed, "or else one of the seals, our poor relations. Boy, now your fate is sealed!" And looking at the wicked seal-faces all around them, George and Jane felt their fate was sealed indeed.

The dwarfs seized the children in their furry arms. George kicked, but it is no use kicking sealskin, and Jane howled, but the dwarfs were getting used to that. They climbed up the dragon's side and dumped the children down on his icy spine, with their backs against the North Pole. You have no idea how cold it was — the kind of cold that makes you feel small and prickly inside your clothes, and makes you wish you had twenty times as many clothes to feel small and prickly inside of.

The sealskin dwarfs tied George and Jane to the North Pole, and, as they had no ropes, they bound them with snow-wreaths, which are very strong when they are made in the proper way, and they heaped up fires very close and said:

"Now the dragon will get warm, and when he gets warm he will wake, and when he wakes he will be hungry, and when he is hungry he will begin to eat, and the first thing he will eat will be *you*."

The little, sharp, many-coloured flames sprang up like the stalks of dream lilies, but no heat came to the children, and they grew colder and colder.

"We shan't be very nice when the dragon does eat us, that's one comfort," said George. "We shall be turned into ice before that."

Suddenly there was a flapping of wings, and the white grouse perched on the dragon's head and said:

"Can I be of any assistance?"

Now by this time the children were so cold, so cold, so very, very cold, that they had forgotten everything but that, and they could say nothing else. So the white grouse said:

"One moment. I am only too grateful for this opportunity of showing my sense of your manly conduct about the firework!"

And the next moment there was a soft whispering rustle of wings overhead, and then, fluttering slowly, softly down, came hundreds and thousands of little white fluffy feathers. They fell on George and Jane like snowflakes, and, like flakes of fallen snow lying one above another, they grew into a thicker and thicker covering, so that presently the children were buried under a heap of white feathers and only their faces peeped out.

"Oh, you dear, good, kind white grouse," said Jane, "but you'll be cold yourself, won't you, now you have given us all your pretty dear feathers?"

The white grouse laughed, and his laugh was echoed by thousands of kind, soft bird-voices.

"Did you think all those feathers came out of one breast? There are hundreds and hundreds of us here, and every one of us can spare a little tuft of soft breast feathers to help to keep two kind little hearts warm!"

Thus spoke the grouse, who certainly had very pretty manners.

So now the children snuggled under the feathers and were warm, and when the sealskin dwarfs tried to take the feathers away, the grouse and his friends

24

flew in their faces with flappings and screams, and drove the dwarfs back. They are a cowardly folk.

The dragon had not moved yet — but then he might at any moment get warm enough to move, and though George and Jane were now warm they were not comfortable, nor easy in their minds. They tried to explain to the grouse; but though he is polite, he is not clever and he only said:

"You've got a warm nest, and we'll see that no one takes it from you. What more could you possibly want?"

Just then came a new, strange, jerky fluttering of wings far softer than the grouse's, and George and Jane cried out together:

"Oh, *do* mind your wings in the fires!"

For they saw at once that it was the great white Arctic moth.

"What's the matter?" he asked, settling on the dragon's tail.

So they told him.

"Sealskin, are they?" said the moth; "just you wait a minute!"

He flew off very crookedly, dodging the flames, and presently he came back, and there were so many moths with him that it was as if a live sheet of white wingedness were suddenly drawn between the children and the stars.

And then the doom of the bad sealskin dwarfs fell suddenly on them.

For the great sheet of winged whiteness broke up and fell, as snow falls, and it fell upon the sealskin dwarfs; and every snowflake of it was a live, fluttering, hungry moth, that buried its greedy nose deep in the sealskin fur.

Grown-up people will tell you that it is not moths but moths' children who eat fur — but this is only when they are trying to deceive you. When they are not thinking about you they say, "I fear the moths have got my ermine tippet," or, "Your poor Aunt Emma had a lovely sable cloak, but it was eaten by moths." And now there were more moths than have ever been together in this world before, all settling on the sealskin dwarfs.

The dwarfs did not see their danger till it was too late. Then they called for camphor and bitter apple, and oil of lavender, and yellow soap and borax; and some of the dwarfs even started to get these things, but long before any of them could get to the chemist's all was over. The moths ate, and ate, and ate, till the sealskin dwarfs, being sealskin throughout, even to the empty hearts of them, were eaten down to the very life — and they fell one by one on the snow and so came to their end. And all round the North Pole the snow was brown with their flat bare pelts.

"Oh, thank you — thank you, darling Arctic moth," cried Jane. "You *are* good. I do hope you haven't eaten enough to disagree with you afterwards!"

Millions of moth-voices answered, with laughter as soft as moth-wings, "We should be a poor set of fellows if we couldn't over-eat ourselves for once in a while — to oblige a friend."

And off they fluttered, and the white grouse flew off, and the sealskin dwarfs were all dead, and the fires went out, and George and Jane were left alone in the dark with the dragon!

"Oh, dear," said Jane, "this is the worst of all!"

"We've no friends left to help us," said George. He never thought that the dragon himself might help them — but then that was an idea that would never have occurred to any boy.

It grew colder and colder and colder, and even under the grouse feathers the children shivered.

Then, when it was so cold that it could not manage to be any colder without breaking the thermometer, it stopped. And then the dragon uncurled himself from round the North Pole, and stretched his long, icy length over the snow, and said:

"This is something like! How faint those fires did make me feel!"

The fact was, the sealskin dwarfs had gone the wrong way to work: the dragon had been frozen so long that now he was nothing but solid ice all through, and the fires only made him feel as if he were going to die.

But when the fires were out he felt quite well, and very hungry. He looked

round for something to eat. But he never noticed George and Jane, because they were frozen to his back.

He moved slowly off, and the snow-wreaths that bound the children to the Pole gave way with a snap, and there was the dragon, crawling south — with George and Jane on his great scaly, icy shining back. Of course the dragon had to go south if he went anywhere, because when you get to the North Pole there is no other way to go. The dragon rattled and tinkled as he went, exactly like the cut-glass chandelier when you touch it, as you are strictly forbidden to do. Of course there are a million ways of going south from the North Pole — so you will own that it was lucky for George and Jane when the dragon took the right way and suddenly got his heavy feet on the great slide. Off he went, full speed between the starry lamps, towards Forest Hill and the Crystal Palace.

"He's going to take us home," said Jane. "Oh, he is a good dragon. I *am* glad!"

And George was rather glad too, though neither of the children felt at all sure of their welcome, especially as their feet were wet, and they were bringing a strange dragon home with them.

They went very fast, because dragons can go uphill as easily as down. You would not understand why if I told you — because you are only in long division at present; yet if you want me to tell you, so that you can show off to other children, I will. It is because dragons can get their tails into the fourth dimension and hold on there, and when you can do that everything else is easy.

The dragon went very fast, only stopping to eat the collector and the sportsman, who were still struggling to go up the slide — vainly, because they had no tails, and had never even heard of the fourth dimension.

And when the dragon got to the end of the slide he crawled very slowly across the dark field beyond the field where there was a bonfire, next to the next-door garden at Forest Hill. He went slower and slower, and in the bonfire field he stopped altogether, and, because the Arctic regions had not got down so far as that, and because the bonfire was very hot, the dragon began to melt, and melt, and melt — and before the children knew what he was doing they found themselves sitting in a large pool of water, and their boots were as wet as wet, and there was not a bit of dragon left!

So they went indoors.

Of course some grown-up or other noticed at once that the boots of George and Jane were wet and muddy, and that they had both been sitting down in a very damp place, so they were sent to bed immediately. It was long past their time, anyhow.

Now, if you are of an inquiring mind — not at all a nice thing in little children who read fairy tales — you will want to know how it is that since the sealskin dwarfs have all been killed, and the fires all been let out, the aurora borealis shines, on cold nights, as brightly as ever.

My dear, I do not know! I am not too proud to own that there are some things I know nothing about — and this is one of them. But I do know that whoever has lighted those fires again, it is certainly not the sealskin dwarfs. They were all eaten by moths — and moth-eaten things are of no use, even to light fires!